ICE CANYON
MONSTER

A GREENLANDIC CLI-FI THRILLER

KEITH ROMMEL

HELLBENDER
BOOKS

an imprint of Sunbury Press, Inc.
Mechanicsburg, PA USA

HELLBENDER BOOKS

an imprint of Sunbury Press, Inc.
Mechanicsburg, PA USA

For information about special discounts for bulk purchases, please contact Sunbury Press Orders Dept. at (855) 338-8359 or orders@sunburypress.com.

To request one of our authors for speaking engagements or book signings, please contact Sunbury Press Publicity Dept. at publicity@sunburypress.com.

ISBN: 978-1-62006-722-2 (Trade paperback)
ISBN: 978-1-62006-442-9 (Mobipocket)

Library of Congress Control Number: 2016947734

FIRST HELLBENDER BOOKS EDITION: April 2018

Product of the United States of America
0 1 1 2 3 5 8 13 21 34 55

Set in Bookman Old Style
Designed by Crystal Devine
Cover by Lawrence Knorr
Edited by Jennifer Cappello

Continue the Enlightenment!

1

SHAMAN

Akutak knelt down on the hard, cold surface of a mountainous ice sheet that overlooked the valley's deep ice canyon. A large rivulet carried fast-moving glacial water, and the sound of the running river was loud enough to reach Akutak even at this altitude.

Located in the interior of Greenland, beneath the ice sheet and river flow, was a canyon that snaked around and reached the Petermann Glacier on the northern coast. The water melt also flowed beneath the ice and was released into the Arctic Ocean.

True to old tradition almost lost throughout the centuries, Akutak wore the skins of animals that were captured for their meat. The skins were sewn together by his wife. She was a skilled seamstress and made him kamiks, trousers and anoraks, gloves and a hat. It was her skill that protected him against the harsh elements and kept him alive.

Knowing she made the clothing, the frigid cold was of no concern; in Greenland it is said a man is what his wife makes him.

Opening the flap of an animal skin sack that was slung over his shoulder, he peered inside and saw what he had placed there before he left home at first light.

The wind whipped and reminded Akutak that where he was was inhospitable and unwelcoming. But still, he continued to move forward with the plan that took him nearly two years to complete; shrouded in silence even to his kin. What he created and what he was about to do was never shared with anyone else. It couldn't be because that was the way.

He carefully reached into his sack and pulled out a hand-sized tupilaq. This carefully handmade avenging monster was created to keep people away from his native land, which was shrinking each year because of global warming.

The shaman began to chant in his native tongue of Inuit. He called forth in a repeated rhythmic sound, reciting his desire to make those who caused it to pay for what his country was suffering. He wanted to instill fear and summoned a beast, large and unstoppable, filled with the rage of his ancestors. This beast would do terrible things to keep people away from Greenland.

He looked at the tupilaq, made the traditional way to ensure its effectiveness; the design represented exactly what he foresaw as being the bringer of fear and order, death, and a reluctance to challenge the waters around Greenland. Made from carved bone, dried and stretched skin, woven hair and sinew, the totem even contained parts from dead children.

Drawing himself close to the ridge, each footfall carefully placed so as not to plunge to his death, his chant continued as he looked over the edge and into the clear water. He held onto the tupilaq, looked at his work one last time to make sure it was good enough, and then held it out and released it over the flowing water.

He watched it fall and make a tiny a splash as it hit the water. The flow carried the tupilaq away. The current dragged and pulled it below the surface, twirled it as it spread the shaman's curse all around, attempting to summon the great avenging monster that would keep others away from his precious Greenland. If his plan worked, it would give his country time to heal.

Akutak turned away, the chant still deep in his throat. He hoped his spell worked, that it was strong enough, and that others wouldn't figure out what he had done this day; at least for a while. He didn't wish to battle anyone or forfeit his life. He wanted his land—his people's land—to be left alone. He wanted to stop the bleeding while he still had a chance to make a difference. And the blood that would be spilled wouldn't be on his hands.

No, because they did it to themselves. He was merely a doctor spreading out the cure. With all responsibility left atop the peak, he began the long journey home. His chant continued until he reached his destination. His actions remained a secret even to his wife.

2

A CURSE COMES FORTH

Buried under ice a mile thick and stretching a mile long is a one-half-mile-deep crevice in the center of the large island of Greenland. It is larger than the Grand Canyon.

The bedrock that bears the weight of the massive ice pack shifted ever so slightly and a crack formed and slowly moved down to the bottom of the chasm where the tupilaq was hung up. A large boulder shook and rolled away as if it were being pushed. The displaced boulder uncovered a large black cave.

Bubbles dribbled out of the black hole and raced upward to rest underneath the sheet of ice. An orange-skinned, rounded face with two rows of large serrated teeth came forward. The large rounded nostrils and big eyes appeared to be pulled back. They had no lids and seemed to rest on the nose.

The giant beast peered into the crystal clear waterway that rushed past him.

A serrated bone bonnet protected gills and a spiny body with protruding spikes atop its back. Thin arms and clawed hands were set in front of the exposed ribcage that bulged from lack of nourishment.

The nostrils moved as it sniffed the water. The monster grabbed either side of the rock opening and it pulled itself out. Set just behind the ribcage, the monster's body had eight tentacles. The massive, muscular tentacles with huge suction cups were pulled close to the body and bunched together, seemingly tangled. In a quick snap, the tentacles straightened and propelled the goliath forward. Forty feet or more of a beast that just wanted to kill as its master commanded darted out into the river.

Kill.

Kill.

Kill.

It traveled through the canyon at impossible speeds. It ate anything that crossed its path, sometimes swallowing its prey whole. Once it reached the Petermann ice shelf, it paused, worked its nostrils at a depth of nearly one thousand feet, and shot out into the Arctic Ocean. It remained close to the ocean floor to get the lay of the land, its eyesight superior and its sense of smell more acute than a bloodhound. It seemed to be looking to find its first target: that which plagues Greenland.

The creature looked up toward the surface. Whatever it saw or smelled, it didn't hesitate. It pumped its tentacles and shot straight up as fast as a bullet from a gun. The speed it moved at made it appear to be just a blur. It cut through the water with its giant mouth open.

3

LIFE'S JOURNEY

The medium-sized fishing vessel called *Life's Journey* bobbed in the water. A crew of four: Boas, Eko, Fina, and Illaq, all the men were best friends and had invested in the boat equally. They had been fishing these waters together for ten years, and through hard work the boat would be paid off at the end of this season.

Fishing was the main source of many people's livelihoods in Greenland, which employed a staggering sixty-five hundred people out of a population of about sixty-thousand people.

The men readied their nylon, grid-like net and cast it overboard in search of cod, halibut, and salmon. The boat trolled the waters and the men waited for it to fill. They prepared to receive the payload, get the fish into the belly of the boat, return to the dock, unload, and get paid. All that to go out and do it again.

A heavy pull on the net made the nylon groan and the boat jerked hard. The men staggered and Eko fell, grunting as he hit the deck. Illaq helped him up and the men moved to see what the cause might be. To their disbelief, the water that surrounded the boat turned red. The men looked at one another, dumbfounded.

Boas ordered the net up and the men heaved with all of their might, moving as quickly as they could. The net had little to no resistance.

"What is going on?" Fina asked. "Never in all my years of fishing have I seen anything like this."

Then another sudden, powerful tug on the net moved *Life's Journey*'s stern and they almost took on water from being tugged down. The violent jerk and motion of being pulled down and popped up tossed Fina overboard, chucking him fifteen feet away from the boat.

The men threw life preservers over and shouted to their friend to grab onto one. They all knew, especially Fina in this moment, that someone couldn't survive very long in water this cold. A minute at the most.

Everything had already gone numb, and his strength was quickly waning as if the water had the power to steal his energy. Although his arms felt like heavy weights, he managed to grab a preserver.

"Hang on, Fina," Illaq said and stepped up on the ledge on the starboard side. He motioned to jump in and Eko grabbed him and pulled him down.

"What the hell are you doing? We already have to worry about getting him out alive," Eko said. "You going in wouldn't help, and it's not heroic. Get yourself together and tend to Fina."

Illaq fell into place, and the three men who remained on board started to pull the line in and began to drag Fina closer to the boat.

"Hang in there, Fina," Illaq shouted. "We will have you out in a moment and give you the heated blanket. You've got to help us! Move your arms and try to kick your legs—it'll help against the cold."

Fina clearly couldn't move or kick what he couldn't feel. As Fina neared the boat, his expression changed from hope to dread.

He didn't look like a man overboard in frigid waters, concerned about hypothermia or determined to escape the blood he found himself floating in. He look worried . . . like he was going to become a part of the blood.

Just then, his mouth opened wide and a primal scream came out before something unseen pulled him under. He disappeared, lost to the other men in the cloudy water of blood and guts, bubbles the only sign left.

"Fina!" Illaq shouted, and chaos erupted on the boat. "You see what you've done? You should have let me go in after him!"

"You would have been pulled under too, Illaq, don't be a fool."

"He's right," Boas said. "You don't know what's going on down there."

The men continued to scramble to find their fallen friend but were helpless to do anything. The water held its secret, and time was quickly running out for Fina. His minute was almost up.

Then, suddenly, Fina popped up some thirty yards away.

"There," Boas said and pointed. They saw him, and Boas worked the engine and pulled the boat up next to their friend. His driving was so precise that the other two men were able to grab Fina under the arms and pull him on board.

His right leg was missing and Fina shouted out in pain. Blood painted *Life's Journey* into a tragic sojourner.

"*Eqalussuaq*," Illaq said and pointed into the water. It was filled with sharks known as the gurry shark. The massive hunter was one of the largest species of shark still alive, comparable only to the great white.

"What are they doing at this depth?"

"Hunger will bring anything to the surface."

"Not these guys! They stay deep."

Boas floored the throttle on the boat and headed for the coast. Illaq found a blanket and applied as much pressure to Fina's leg as he could. Eko grabbed the warming blanket and worked on pulling off Fina's clothing. Fina grunted in pain, always tough, but hypothermia and shock were a real danger as the men worked on him.

"Hurry!" Illaq shouted over the roar of the engine.

"I'm going as fast as she'll move us," Boas shouted back. "Stay with him and don't let him close his eyes!"

"Eqalussuaq," Fina mumbled. His blue lips and pure white skin were an indication that hypothermia was indeed setting in.

"Yes, the mad beast got you good," Illaq said. "But we're going to get you to a hospital. Get you fixed up. You just need to concentrate on staying awake."

Fina patted his friend's hand, knowing he was in trouble. He tried not to think about the pain or the cold that was deep inside his body. He knew the injury was bad but didn't want to look. The blood all around was enough. He was better off not knowing.

Instead, he wanted to tell Illaq about the strange bright orange thing he saw when he was pulled under. He looked at it with his own two eyes, and he if hadn't seen it himself, he would think the person who told of the encounter had gone mad.

The pain brought blackness, and Fina sought it, knowing that place was much better than this. He could tell his tale later if he survived the trip home.

A slap shook his head, but he didn't care. He wanted to go where he was being called.

The frenzied sharks appeared to be about ten to twenty-one feet long and had the thickest hide of any shark species and also the most inedible meat. The massive fish had short, rounded snouts, small eyes, and tiny dorsal and pectoral fins. The creamy-gray or blackish-brown gurries continued a frenzy of the fish that had been torn from the net. It seemed, indeed, that hunger had brought them up from the depths.

The sharks rolled and wagged their caudal keels and caudal fins to get their fill, seeming to wrestle with their own kind to find proper positioning among the crazed bunch.

Then without warning, the Tupilaq Octopus came up from underneath them for a second time and scooped three of the large predators into its mouth in one pass. The momentum propelled the goliath out of the water and onto its side as it rent the sharks to shreds of meat with its serrated teeth. The creature made a third and final pass and fed on all remaining sharks. Once it was finished, it dove deep, its hunger only beginning, its strength building, its mind sharpening.

4

GLOBAL WARMING?

The massive feeder called the *Wave Cuttur* plodded along through the rough waves of the Baffin Bay, a shipping lane between Canada and Greenland. The massive ship, which had a full load of truck-sized intermodal containers, barely had a sway to it. The cargo pressed the massive ship down into the water. The deck was full and the powerful diesel engines worked hard to spin the giant propellers located in the center and at the tail end of the boat, moving the impossible weight through a current that pushed against the ship.

Despite lower carbon dioxide emissions, burning diesel fuel helped to promote global warming more so than gasoline cars. One massive ship, such as the *Cuttur*, would equal about fifty million cars in the course of a year. The ship and others like it emitted cancer- and asthma-causing pollutants and generated five-thousand-two-hundred tons of sulfur dioxide pollution a year. Over sixty-thousand premature deaths were said to come from diesel emissions each year, and yet the ships kept coming. Larger, faster, more emissions. The Northwest Passage was a busy travel route for container ships that came out of the Chukchi Sea and into the Beaufort Sea, where the mighty ships made their way between Canada and Greenland and ultimately into the Baffin Bay.

The ship caught the attention of the Tupilaq Octopus. Its tentacles worked beneath the surface as it kept its eyes just above the waterline.

The Tupilaq Octopus could smell the airborne pollution from the giant engines—the same pollution that had been linked to coastal sickness by residents near busy shipping lanes such as Baffin Bay.

The Tupilaq Octopus sank below the surface, the emotion of the creature that of anger. It hovered while it watched the belly of the ship and the propellers churn up the waters above it. Before it dove deep it looked up at the vessel and assessed it.

5

HE'S AWAKE

The three men from *Life's Journey* waited to hear word on Fina's condition. When they got him to the hospital, he was in and out of consciousness, mumbling about something orange. He had lost a tremendous amount of blood and the men thought he was hallucinating; dying from blood loss and hypothermia.

Not a single word was said among the men as they waited for the doctor, each of them stained with Fina's blood, his screams and his pleas.

Boas, Eko, and Illaq hoped for the best and were told they would hear from the surgeon soon. "Soon" had been an hour ago so far. But they knew how severe his injuries were, and however long the doctor needed to save their friend's life he could have, and they would wait in the silence they were blanketed in.

"Gentleman," a man said as he emerged through a door that made no sound. He wore blue scrubs and had a tied rag over his hair. "Your friend is a strong man, and although his condition remains critical, he's awake and is asking to see you all."

"That's wonderful," Illaq said.

"More like a miracle," the doctor said. "I'm granting him special permission to see you guys. You have to cover up with some disposable suits and masks we'll provide you with. Although it is dressed, I don't want any contaminants getting into his wound. You have ten minutes with him from the moment you get into his room. Ten minutes. What he needs most right now is rest, but a visit from his friends might do him some good."

"Thank you, Doctor," Eko said.

The doctor nodded. "Be mindful he's on morphine for the pain and may seem a little out of it. We have a heated blanket on him to keep his body heat up."

"Yes, thank you, Doctor," Boas said.

Illaq was choked up.

"You're welcome."

"It's going to be OK," Eko said and put an arm around Illaq. "We're just happy to be able to see him. He made it through it."

"He's hallucinating from the drugs a little, and he rambles sometimes about things that don't make much sense. I don't know anything about your job, but he's talking some really weird stuff so be ready for it."

The doctor walked away.

Fina watched the men he had worked with for half his life on *Life's Journey* walk into the room. Tears filled his eyes and a somber expression was on their faces.

"Fina," Boas said.

"I lost my leg all the way up," Fina said. "I don't think I'll be fishing with you guys ever again."

"That's nonsense," Boas said. "You get the wheelhouse and I'll take the deck. It was your turn anyway. You need to understand that me and the boys aren't leaving you on land. You belong in the sea and on that boat."

"That's right. There's no chance you're staying on the sidelines," Eko said.

"You're too important to the crew," Illaq said. "You bled all over us. That means you owe us."

Fina smiled but the tears came. The smile took over as he wiped his eyes.

"Don't start getting all soft on us now," Boas said. "You stared one of the most deadly fish in the waters in the eyes and you survived."

"About that," Fina said. He fell silent and looked at each one of his friends. "There's something I have to tell you guys, and I want you to listen to what I have to say."

"Why don't you wait until tomorrow to tell us? The doctor says you need your rest and he gave us a strict ten minutes. He said that you're on heavy medication and we need to let you rest," Eko said.

"No," Fina said. He reached out and touched Boas' hand. "What I need to say is important, and you need to hear it before you go."

The men looked at each other as if unsure if what he was about to say was a truth or a hallucination brought on by heavy doses of medication.

"Sure, Fina, OK. What is it?" Illaq said.

"It was the eqalussuaq that took me under. That shark was big and I looked her right in the eye as she bit into my leg. She took me down, let me go, grabbed me again, and took me down some more. Even though I couldn't feel it because my body was numb, I knew it should hurt. I took a small breath of water. I was giving up."

"We don't need to hear this right now," Eko said. "The doctor said you need your rest. We are going to go, let you be. We'll be back tomorrow."

"No!" Fina shouted. He looked at his hands . . . and then at the place where his leg should be. It was amazing how he had no pain. "I saw something under there . . . under the eqalussuaq. It was massive and it moved so fast I could barely see it. It was orange and it came up under the belly of the shark. Whatever that thing was, that's what ate that shark in one bite and took my leg that was in its mouth with it."

"Fina," Illaq said and placed a hand on Fina's forearm and gave it a gentle squeeze. "Rest, my friend."

"I will, but you have to hear me out. You have to hear this just in case."

"Just in case of what?" Boas said.

Fina just looked at them. "You know. Don't make me say it."

"You're not going anywhere. You've made it through the worst part of it. Besides, you're too stubborn."

"We're listening."

"I ended up getting tossed while the beast chomped down on the eqalussuaq and me. It spit me out of harm's way. It happened as the creature turned and took the eqalussuaq into the deep. It had tentacles, and when the goliath pumped its tentacles, the wave of water it displaced was what tossed me away. I spun around in the water with no sense of what was happening to me. I didn't know if I was going down or up. Well, I popped up and that's why you guys were able to spot me. That's also the reason why you had to come get me so far away from where I went under."

A nurse came into the room. "You gentlemen have to leave now. Fina needs his rest."

"It happened as it pumped its appendages to go wherever it was headed. Did you hear what I said?"

"Yes, we heard what you said. Rest now, Fina," Illaq said.

"Yes, rest up, my friend," Eko said.

"You guys need to understand the sheer size of this thing. It was bigger than anything I've ever seen down there," Fina called out as his friends exited the room.

"I wonder if he saw what he says," Illaq said.

"What he saw was a shark—an eqalussuaq," Boas said. "He's still in shock . . . trying to understand what happened."

"It's like the doctor said," Eko said. "He has a lot of medication in him. He didn't even seem like he was in any sort of pain and he had his leg torn from his body only six hours ago. Think about that."

Illaq nodded his head. "It's hard to know if what he was saying was the truth. But I did see in his eyes he believed what he was saying. He had a genuine belief that he saw something big and orange."

"What if he said it was a mermaid? Would you believe it then?" Boas asked.

"No, I suppose not," Illaq said.

"We will wait until tomorrow. Maybe he'll be more clear headed then. We can talk to him when he is a bit more clear headed."

The three men exited the hospital. They wanted to get out of their bloodstained clothing. Normally it wouldn't bother them to have blood on them because it would be from the fish. But to have their friend's blood on them was something else entirely.

6

CONTAINER SHIP

The Tupilaq Octopus followed the *Wave Cuttur* container ship. It remained about fifty feet below the hull, and the massive eyes that appeared as though they looked straight ahead really looked at the four massive propellers that twirled and sliced through the water. The cavitation caught the Tupilaq Octopus' attention as did the booming sound of the propellers.

The Tupilaq Octopus picked a spot and ascended to the center of the ship. It used four of its powerful, thick arms and suctioned them to the flat steel surface and dug its clawed hands into the hull with a firm hold. The drag of the ocean water was of no consequence to the creature's might. It watched the propellers spin, cleave the water, and scream with sound that it despised.

The four remaining tentacles inched along the bottom of the boat and slowly made their way to the shaft of the propeller, wrapped it, and held it, squeezing harder and harder.

The propeller stopped spinning and the tentacles remained firm in their hold until the resistance from the shaft stopped too. The monster then grabbed onto the thick blade tips and bent them flat.

The tentacles moved to the next shaft and repeated the same process. But this time when it went to bend the blade tips, the massive amount of strength behind the crushing force of the four tentacles snapped the shaft and the propeller sank into the deep.

With two of the four propellers out of commission, the Tupilaq Octopus moved to the two remaining propellers, cinched the shafts, bent the blade tips, and unlatched from the ship that was now at the mercy of the slapping waves in the wide open ocean.

7

MAYDAY

Four men were in drysuits. Each had their own breathing tubes handled by someone topside, a functioning camera system on top of the full cover face mask, and even a communication system radioed to topside. They were lowered into the water via crane with special care to move them far enough away from the ship in case a rogue wave came along. The water could take a man and slam him on the side of the *Wave Cuttur* and kill him instantly.

It took the team nearly an hour to get into the frigid water and inspect the underside of the huge ship. They secured themselves to the bottom of the ship with strong suction cups that attached with a twist. They could crawl along the bottom of the ship and not have to worry about the movement of the ship. Each man was assigned to a specific propeller.

When the first man reached his destination, he radioed in. "Topside, are you seeing what I'm seeing?"

Static came back and the diver repeated himself while he looked at the broken, twisted shaft and missing propeller. He glanced down into the deep and saw nothing but blackness.

"We're seeing it," a voice came back, the disbelief clearly shared.

"You recording the feeds topside?"

"All of them," the staticky response came back. "We're waiting on the others. Please return topside."

The diver let air out of his suit, disengaged from the boat, and descended an easy thirty feet rapidly at a safe distance to keep the swaying and dipping boat from coming down on top of him. He swam clear of the *Wave Cuttur* and watched the other men working. He didn't like what he saw.

He stopped swimming close enough to the ship that the crane could reach him.

"I'm clear, Topside, and ready to come aboard."

The man was hoisted up.

The second and third men reached their targets at the same time.

"Diver two coming up on the prop," he said and slowly crawled along the hull of the ship, absorbing every dip and sway as if he were a spring. "Topside, is my camera operating?"

"It is," Topside came back.

"Topside, this is diver three looking at something unexplainable," he said. Nervousness overtook him and he began to search the depths below.

"Divers two and three return topside."

The radio man switched frequencies to communicate with diver four.

"Diver four return topside. We're dead in the water."

"Roger that," he released air from his suit, too, and dropped deep below the ship. "I was having a hell of a time navigating the tide while I was connected to the *Wave Cuttur*. It's like we're in a slow spin or something."

"We are," com came back.

The three remaining divers dove to a depth of fifty feet, saw the mangled propellers, and gave com a good look at the devastation with their mask-mounted cams. One of the men was nervous at the thought of what could have done this. The diver looked down and caught a glimpse of massive orange tentacles disappearing into the deep. There was no doubt he had just seen a monstrous creature.

The sheer size of the creature would make anyone fearful if they were to witness it. He panicked, worried it was coming back, and the diver screamed into his mask.

"I just saw a fucking giant squid or octopus or something!" He broke away and made a mad dash to get himself to the surface. "The thing is as big as this boat!" He continued his rapid ascent.

The boat dipped and hit him. His neck broke instantly. He was dragged along by the unpredictable current. The only things stopping him from drifting out to sea were his oxygen hoses.

The two remaining divers didn't see what he saw and made their way past the *Wave Cuttur* and began their safe ascent toward the ship's deck. After a few moments, they arrived safely topside. The dead man was pulled up by his oxygen lines, men heaving him up, his body limp.

"Come," one of the deckhands said to the divers.

"What of Ikaana?" one of the divers said.

"He's dead. The *Wave Cuttur* came down on top of him. He broke protocol and didn't stand a chance."

"What did he swim from? Please tell me you caught whatever he saw! What could do that to an experienced diver and mangle our propellers like that?"

"The captain wants you in the wheelhouse so you can see."

They hurried to the wheelhouse and to the com station, the weight of their dead comrade already weighing heavily on their shoulders. But adrenaline took over; the men needed to see.

There was a video, paused, awaiting their arrival.

"You need to see what Ikaana's cam caught."

The man hit play, and first the devastation to the propellers was played. Then a grainy video of the deep water below revealed a secret. It looked like massive octopus tendrils that dove deep, and the sight brought everyone closer to the monitor.

"Look at the size of that thing!"

"No wonder Ikaana freaked out."

"But he knew better, dammit."

"That thing may very well be what is responsible for mangling our props."

"There is no doubt about it."

"This is the *Wave Cuttur* calling in from . . ."

The men turned away, leaving the captain to send out the distress signal. They made their way to Ikaana's body and knelt over him.

"Whatever that thing is, it's responsible for killing him."

"Maybe all of us if help doesn't get here soon."

"We're a floating box in a violent bathtub."

The men disconnected Ikaana's breathing tubes and took their man below deck. They wrapped his body in a blanket and put it in the large walk-in refrigerator. They set him down upon an empty shelf. They knelt beside him, one at a time, and paid their respects.

"We should hunt that thing. Kill it for what it has done."

"That thing tore a propeller off this boat and bent the others, collapsing them like they were made of tin. We can't hunt whatever it is we saw. Something like that hunts us, and I don't think we're safe on this ship."

8

FINA

Illaq, Boas, and Eko stood around Fina's bed. He looked better this day. The color in his face had returned, and although he was still on the drip, they had lessened the dosage and his awareness seemed sharp. The heated blanket had been removed, and that made the stump of his missing leg more obvious and hard not to look at.

"How are you feeling today, Fina?" Eko said.

"Don't give me sympathy here. I wouldn't give it to you, so let's skip the crap here, guys, and let's talk about what I was trying to tell you yesterday," Fina said. "Damn nurse kicked you out right in the middle of it."

"All right," Boas said and folded his arms across his chest. "You make no mention that you're missing a leg and don't seem to care that we are worried for you. Why must you harp on the struggle that took your leg?"

"My leg is gone, Boas, and there's not a thing I can do about that. It's in the belly of a beast. And I'm not talking about a gurry shark, either. Yes, I am still in some pain, and when I look down and see that my leg is missing I swear I can still feel it. It is the weirdest thing. But you guys need to know what I saw and find a way to believe me. I'm concerned about people's safety."

Illaq stepped closer to Fina's bed. "Tell us then. Tell us what you saw with your own eyes."

"I saw a giant sea creature." He paused. "No, it was a monster. It was something so big it could devour a container ship. Snap a large vessel in half. And it was orange in color. It was fast. So very fast."

The men looked at each other and an awkward silence filled the room. Eyes returned to Fina, and he looked uncomfortable having been stuck in the bed and unable to get away from their stares.

"What? Stop looking at me like that." His gaze swung from person to person. "All of you."

"Well then keep going, Fina. Tell us your story. We want to hear what you have to say," Eko said. "You said it was important."

"From what I could see, this creature looked like an octopus. I could see thick tendrils, and it had suction cups bigger than my head. It was only a snapshot as I was torn and tossed. My eyes, they saw this beast, and it is seared into my mind."

"There's something we need to tell you," Boas said.

"I dreamt about it last night. I know what I saw."

"We believe you."

Fina remained silent; his hands shook and his eyes were wide as quarters, expectant as to what he was about to be told.

"A container ship was attacked yesterday not too long after the incident on *Life's Journey*."

"Attacked how?"

"All four propellers were targeted; bent beyond recognition. One of them was torn off the ship completely. Divers went down when it seemed like they were having mechanical issues. They had head cams rolling and they caught a glimpse of this octopus you describe. It's exactly as you say, Fina. They have a five second clip of massive tendrils with suction cups and a creature diving deep at an unbelievable speed."

"Oh my . . ." Fina swallowed hard. "I thought I was hallucinating it at first. The dream I was talking about . . . it kept waking me all night." He lifted his head up and looked at his friends. "You guys can't

go back out there until they find out what it is.
Life's Journey is to remain docked."

"That's not all, Fina."

"What do you mean that's not all?" He looked at
everyone again. Their faces were sorrowful, none
wanting to say what was coming next.

"The container ship that was attacked was the
Wave Cuttur."

Fina looked at his friends. "Tell me they sent a
helicopter and got everyone off the crippled ship!"

"They did, Fina. The boat is adrift and tugs
should be arriving there as we speak to try and get
her into port."

"Well that's good."

Eko nodded his head. "Yeah, that's good.
Remember when we told you they had footage of the
props all bent up and one was missing?"

"Yeah."

"Ikaana was one of the divers to check below the
ship. He is the one that caught those images. But it
is said he panicked when he saw it and ascended
too quickly, straight up. The *Cuttur* hit a wave and
came down on top of him."

"What?" Fina's eyes welled with tears. "Is he OK?
Were they able to help him?"

Illaq shook his head. "No, Fina, they weren't. He died from the heavy blow of the ship."

Fina started to cry. "I told him I didn't want him on those things but he wouldn't listen! Now I'm left alone to mourn the loss myself and deal with the fact that I'm missing my damn leg!"

"You're not alone."

"To hell I ain't."

"You're not. And although we don't know what you're feeling, we will be here for you every step of the way," Eko said. "You will not mourn alone, and you will not be left to fend for yourself. We will be there. We are like family."

"That's right," Illaq said.

"But that's my little brother who died out there . . . smashed to bits by a ship."

"We know, Fina, and we're sorry we had to tell you."

Fina cried hard and his friends remained at his side like they promised.

9

TUGGED

Two integral unit tugboats arrived at the helpless *Wave Cuttur*. They attached to the ship with giant tethers, one in the rear of the container ship, the other in the front. Once the ship was secure, they began to maneuver the stranded vessel toward the closest harbor. One boat pushed and the other pulled; their engines worked at full capacity, making the water behind them look like it was boiling.

A helicopter above helped communicate with the tugs and their captains. The rough seas made it difficult for the poor sea-keeping tugs to maneuver, but the smaller crafts worked hard. These two tugs were all the Greenlandic government was afforded by Iceland. They didn't want the container ship that was left adrift to succumb to the treacherous sea and unforgiving waves. That would be a disaster of epic proportions.

The tug in the front began to stall and the pilot of the helicopter tried to transmit what he saw. The copilot was of no help, paralyzed by what he saw. He could only watch as the bright orange octopus came beneath the stout boat and wrapped its eight tentacles around it in a strong embrace. The monster dwarfed the boat. It squeezed and jerked downward. The boat went under but came back up. Cracked almost in half, it began to take on water. With a second jerk from the massive tendrils, the boat was torn in half and began to sink. The men in the water were scooped up by the tendrils and dragged below the surface.

The Tupilaq Octopus turned its attention to the rear tug and rammed into it, pulled on it, broke the winch and tether, and pulled it along and then left it alone to drift. The Tupilaq disappeared into the depths as if it seemed disinterested.

Moments later the giant beast returned and capsized the boat. It flung the men around with its tentacles, and the prehistoric face maddened as it opened its great maw and fed on those who tried to stay above the water, finishing them with one easy gulp. Then it was gone.

The men in the helicopter looked down on the broken chaos, unsure how they could explain what they saw and what sort of devastation was left out here. Anyone who dared to enter the water would face the monster that quite possibly came from the deepest part of the sea. And it seemed no matter what they had, they wouldn't survive more than the creature wanted them to. They circled the devastation and checked the waters for any possible survivors. Everything was debris. All the men were dead. What they saw was impossible to shake.

The pilot flew to the harbor; his copilot was pinned to his seat, his face a mask of terror. The pilot knew shock had set in. The man he had flown with and relied on through difficult situations for years had become a shell. A husk of trauma frozen in time. He realized, it's a hell of a thing to imagine seeing a monster come out of a closet or out from underneath a bed but so different to see it emerge from the sea and create such devastation.

10

COMMUNICATION

TELE Greenland broadcast through radio, television, fixed and mobile phones, as well as the Internet. The message that was delivered said as follows:

"We are looking into reports of a possible sea creature wreaking havoc off our coast. This creature is said to be an octopus that's the size of a container ship, possibly larger. As farfetched as this might be, we take all claims seriously for the safety of our people. Greenlandics are to use caution until these claims can be fully investigated and validated or dismissed.

"We understand the ocean is where most of you earn your livelihood and we caution you to stay out of the water. Although we are unsure if the claims are true, as we've only been given grainy images and the accounts from people who have come forward, the stories have some consistency. Meanwhile, others seem to contradict and exaggerate. We will not comment about human fatalities or specific incidents surrounding this alleged monster for the protection of the families involved.

"More news to come as it becomes available to us through actual scientific evaluation and physical investigation."

11

WHEN ALL IS LOST

Fina shut the television off, tossed the remote aside, and closed his eyes. He could see the tentacles. They were thick and strong and as real as the missing appendage the creature took away from him. He didn't want to think about what it did to his brother. It brought forth a swirling anger deep in his chest that only dissipated in dashes of distracted and drastic thoughts.

The government needed proof—they had all they needed floating out in the sea and from someone lying in bed, broken and ruined on the outside and in. Who else knew what the government had that they weren't telling people? They would sit on this and would hope if they ignored it, it would just go away.

But Fina knew it wouldn't. That monster was out to troll the waters around Greenland and make anyone pay for reasons he didn't yet understand.

This thing was a mindless killing machine. A creation from hell.

Although Fina long ago left the practice of being a shaman, he had an idea of what had to be done to neutralize the threat. It was the only thing that made sense. Of course he would have to keep what he was doing a secret. That was the only way a shaman worked his magic. Now he was at war with an enemy he didn't know. Another shaman was responsible for that abomination. Fina was sure of it. He was nervous and confident all at the same time.

Taking the risk of doing battle had its reward. He could return the favor and avenge his brother's death. But he would have to do it right, because if he didn't, it would cost him much more than a leg or his ire for losing a sibling—it would cost him his life. He had only one chance at this and needed to be smart in his approach.

12

THE SHAMAN

Akutak released his tupilaq yesterday, and the monster he conjured had already disabled a shipping vessel and sunk two tugboats. The statement was being made that it was not safe in the waters around Greenland. Soon, he hoped, the shipping lanes would be closed down because any captain foolish enough to enter the waters that surrounded the country and spew emissions and make his people sick and his ice recede would know Greenland now had a protector.

A big one that was fierce. Fearless. Mighty.

Akutak found a mid-sized mound in the otherwise flat area and he gently went to his knees, then lay prone. He spied the herd of muskox with their thick brown coats swaying in the steady beating wind. He aimed his .45-70 Marlin lever action rifle, choosing the closest one.

"I thank you, Lord, for this gift."

He took aim and fired the weapon. It was a good shot. The muskox fell where it stood.

He went to his kill, saw it was still alive, and chambered a bullet to put the animal down with one to the head.

The meat would go a long way in helping to feed people in his village, and the fur would go to his wife, Sarmok, to make more clothing and blankets. Their one-year-old daughter, Ronja, could also use a doll.

As Akutak gutted the beast, he thought about what he had done yesterday. Although the government controlled communications and said there wasn't definitive proof of a large monster's existence, people knew the truth. They knew something was out there. News traveled fast within the communities all along the coast. He wanted as few casualties of his fellow Greenlandics as possible. He knew some would succumb to the monster but hoped the body count would be very little. If they looked at the Tupilaq Octopus' actions it would be easy to see why the beast was created. It was not evil and was worthy of life in the seas around Greenland.

It should have been created years ago, but Akutak lacked the skills to bring forth such a thing.

There was nervousness in his heart. If other shamans would figure things out, too, they wouldn't try to counteract what he set in motion and he would be safe. But if another shaman was to create another tupilaq, he might be in trouble. Another shaman was the only one capable of stopping the Tupilaq Octopus.

But that shaman had to be able to conjure a more powerful tupilaq. If he didn't, he would face the curse of death. If he did, Akutak would face the same. There was a chance he might not ever see his wife or precious daughter again. She was the cutest thing in the world, and her birth changed him in ways that nothing else could. However, his dear daughter wasn't in danger—at least not now that his Tupilaq was around to rescue his melting country.

Akutak knew the risk he had taken when he started to create his tupilaq and when he finished it and dropped it over the side of the ice mountain and into the frigid water. The only way to avoid death associated with what he'd done was to admit his secret act before his conjured creature was defeated. He wasn't sure he wanted to embarrass his family with the admission that he dabbled in the dark arts.

He went ahead and tried to quiet his mind and worked on gutting the muskox and salvaging all he could. He needed to work fast as the biting cold would freeze the body quickly and he would have to work twice as hard to pillage the things he needed from the beautiful animal.

13

A SHIP AND AN OCTOPUS

A fully loaded boat, like the last ship that tried to pass through, carried truck-sized, intermodal containers through Baffin Bay. The ship's name was the *Gentle Giant*, and it cut through the waves easily. The propellers underneath the water worked hard at pushing the liquid so that the ship could move forward.

Diesel engines spewed emissions into the air; this ship was bigger, stronger, and faster than the *Wave Cuttur*.

Deep below the surface, the Tupilaq Octopus was resting in its cave deep in the canyon below the ice in the center of the country. Its acute hearing picked up on the sound and it exited the cave and pumped its massive tentacles, pushing the octopus at a speed twenty times that of what it was now after.

Energized from all the food it had consumed, it wasted no time following the sound and stopping deep below the moving vessel. The trail of white water the propellers left was filled with bubbles and foam.

It stared.

It hovered.

It found rage that was placed there by Akutak regarding the pollution these ships were causing.

The eight legs bunched close to the body and were slithering like a snake, swaying, waiting as the ship neared and moved over the top of it. The legs shot out and the Tupilaq Octopus darted straight up, headed for the belly of the container ship.

The massive mouth opened to show two rows of razor sharp teeth, and it pushed the quickly flowing water out of its gills, which were set behind a protective bone bonnet. The rounded mouth, setback eyes, and wide nostrils set just above the nose rippled in the water from the great speed.

With the force of a torpedo being shot out of a submarine, the Tupilaq Octopus slammed into the bottom of the container vessel. It lifted it out of the water, and the giant ship swayed and dropped back down with a heavy splash. Some of the containers on board fell into each other, the tethers that secured them snapping from the sheer force of the collision. The Tupilaq bit into the steel hull, its jaws squashing the thick steel like it were made of soft flesh. It shook its head and tore a chunk out of the vessel.

The Tupilaq took the metal from its mouth, crumpled it in its hands, and then went after the engines. One by one it crippled the ship, seizing the propellers, bending them beyond use or repair. The ship, like the *Wave Cuttur*, was disabled.

As the hole in the bottom center of the vessel filled with water, the Tupilaq entered the ship and found some dead bodies. It fed. The entire ship wouldn't flood and sink because the remaining crew had managed to seal off the portion of the vessel that the Tupilaq had destroyed and entered.

The beast sat in the hole. It wanted to sink the boat the way it did the tugs, but it knew the pollution that would spill into the sea would be a disaster. That would be doing more harm than good and going against its creator's wishes.

It exited the hole, climbed the side of the ship, and used its tentacles to straddle the large boat and crush the cargo. It growled and screamed at the people, who were badly shaken up, opening its massive arms and looking skyward as it sent them scrambling for safety. It picked up a trailer and slammed it down, crushing it and shaking the vessel.

A tentacle moved through the tangle of cargo and found the wheelhouse. It wrapped the rectangular control room in its strategically placed suction cups so they had a secure, strong hold. The monster pulled. The wheelhouse bent forward, the welded steel cracked and split, and the control room looked down at the deck. The people inside were tossed around.

The monster stayed, let everyone get a good look at what it was, and then it simply let go of the crippled boat and slid into the water. It dove deep below the surface, looking for something else to take its anger out on.

14

A SECRET

Boas, Illaq, and Eko all said they would go to the hospital in the morning to hang out with Fina. Illaq was the first to arrive. His face was red from the cold, and as he entered the room he wore an artificial smile that didn't bother Fina.

"How are you feeling today?" Illaq said.

"I'm feeling a little better." He picked at his fingernails. "The doctors have lowered the dosage of my medication even more and the nurses come in every few hours to change the bandages."

"That's good. They're keeping it clean making sure infection doesn't set in."

"Yeah," Fina said and looked at the wall to his right. He wished there was a window there. He was going crazy being caught in this room, married to this bed with nothing to look at.

"They said I won't be able to attend Ikaana's funeral."

"I'm sorry," Illaq said and Fina knew he was. "We are going and we will represent you."

Fina didn't answer.

"Is there anything I can get you?" Illaq said and paused while he waited for an answer.

"In fact there is," Fina said, his sadness transformed into determination. "But what I ask of you, I need you to keep quiet about it. Can you do that?"

"What is it?"

"That doesn't matter. What matters is I need it, and I need to know you'll make two promises to me because I'm trusting you by asking you to do this for me."

"OK, what is it?"

"In my bedroom, underneath my bed, is a shoebox. It is very old and things inside will rattle and slide around. The first promise is, as tempting as it might be, don't open the lid and look inside. Second promise is don't tell the guys about it. In fact, I'd like you to wait until they leave for you to give it to me. After you get it, you have to go so I can examine its contents."

"What's—"

"Don't," Fina said and raised a hand. "I'm not going to tell you. You either make the promises and tell me you can do this or I'm going to ask someone else."

It was Illaq's turn to remain in silence.

"You're my best friend. You helped me from bleeding out and you're the first one here like I knew you would be."

"When do you want me to go and get this?"

"Now," Fina said. "Take my keys out of my jeans over there in the bag on the floor. Can you feed the dogs while you're there?"

"We're already taking care of the dogs."

Fina smiled. "Yes, of course. Thank you for that. Are you letting them out of their cages? Playing with them?"

"We are and wonder sometimes how they can stand the cold."

"That's where they have remained since they were pups. You know that."

"I feel bad."

"They have a home and a master who loves them."

"I know they do."

"Make sure you come back with something for me."

"Like what?"

"A candy bar, donut, ice cream . . . anything that'll explain why you're late and to keep suspicion away from what you're doing for me."

"This isn't going to hurt anyone is it?"

"Like who?"

"Yourself?" He shrugged. "I don't know, how do I know there's not a gun in there? Or poison or something?"

Fina laughed. "It's nothing like that. I don't want to hurt myself or anyone else. I promise you that."

"OK."

"See? A promise for a promise. You're one up on me so I owe you."

"You don't owe me anything."

Illaq rummaged through the bag, then the pockets of the jeans, and found the keys. He shoved them into his pocket and went to exit the room when Boas and Eko arrived.

"Hey, Fina, how are you doing today?" Boas said.

"I was just telling Illaq that the doctors reduced the medication. I hardly have pain and the nurses come in here every few hours and change the bandages."

"Oh," Eko said and elbowed Boas. "He's probably got some pretty ones."

"Hey guys," Illaq said. "I'll be back in a little bit."

"Where are you going?"

"I'm heading out to get Fina a nice hot cup of coffee."

"The hospital coffee is like drinking toilet water," Fina interjected.

"I'll see you guys in a little while."

"OK," Boas said. "Maybe you can bring one back for me and Eko?"

"All right, I can do that."

"I don't want one," Eko said and sat in the chair next to the bed.

Illaq exited the room.

"Has there been anything new about the cargo ship that was attacked yesterday?" Fina asked.

"They sent two tugboats out yesterday to try and push the thing to the docks but word is going around from some helicopter pilot that a massive octopus attacked the tugs," Boas said. "It snapped one of the ships in half and capsized the other."

"It's also being said that whatever they saw out there, the copilot is catatonic," Eko said. "That tells me they saw something awful."

"The pilot described the beast as being as big as the large ship, with huge tentacles, and of course, orange in color. It's making no attempt to hide its existence. The upper portion of the body is supposed look lizard-like. Big round mouth, huge eyes and nose, with a bone bonnet at the back of its head. Then the rear turns into an octopus. The thing is real prehistoric."

"Sounds like what might have attacked the shark that had me, don't you think?" Fina looked at them both. "The thing that scared my brother so bad that he didn't think about his ascent right underneath the ship that killed him?"

Boas and Eko looked at each other.

"Don't tell me you didn't put that together."

Boas pressed his back against the wall and slid down until he was sitting. "What is this thing?"

"I don't know," Fina said. "I've been trying to figure that out all night."

"What does it want?" Boas said.

"It sounds like a mad beast creating havoc around our island, doesn't it?" Eko said.

"Maybe," Fina said. "But why?"

"We should gather a bunch of men, get the biggest boat we can find, and hunt it," Boas said. "We need to kill it."

"No!" Fina said and sat up. "Don't you dare go into those waters. Do you hear me?"

Boas stood. "We can't let this thing just attack everything without fighting back. It took your leg and killed your brother."

"I know what it did," Fina said. "But that thing out there . . . what I saw . . . that thing is a fight for someone else."

Boas went quiet.

"Hey," Fina shouted. "Did you hear what I said?"

"Yeah, I heard you."

"I don't like when you get quiet. It means you're thinking about it. Don't. Get it through your head that this thing is snapping tugs in half and dismantling container ships. What do you have that's going to stop it?"

Boas nodded in acceptance.

"We have a government refusing to acknowledge it," Eko said. "You saw it. Maybe you should come forward . . . tell them what you saw."

"No," Fina said. "I was attacked by an eqalussuaq. A shark. I don't want you guys saying anything more than that to anyone. Do you understand me?"

Eko and Boas reluctantly agreed.

"OK."

"Fine."

Fina rested his head on his pillow, his eyes filled with tears. "It's not your fight. Remember that. It's too big and powerful for you. I know you want to kill it because of what happened. Let's not talk about it. Let me heal here." Fina tapped his temple.

15

INTELLIGENCE

The massive, eight-legged Tupilaq Octopus entered the Baffin Bay. The sound of three powerful propellers from outboard engines churned the water behind *The Mistress of the Sea*. It made the creature pump its tentacles, moving in to investigate and possibly disable the ship. It was learning from sound what it needed to go after, but this—this was different.

There was a smell, something putrid in the clean waters that it trolled. The smell was old but everywhere and it confused the Tupilaq.

The creature from the deep caught up to the *The Mistress of the Sea*, this hull much smaller than the others. It watched from deep below the surface as three even smaller crafts with outboard engines came into view and rode next to the *The Mistress of the Sea*.

The Tupilaq watched the smaller, much faster ships that swarmed around *The Mistress of the Sea*. In its confusion to understand, the Tupilaq Octopus looked around and saw something hulking that came down from above and invaded the ocean floor.

There were four massive galvanized steel legs that dug their feet into the rock, sand, silt, and clay that made up the ocean floor. In the center, a large pipe penetrated the surface.

That was where the smell was coming from. It was the rock below the surface in distress: burnt and broken, nature's beauty violated where it shouldn't be.

The Tupilaq Octopus grabbed onto *The Mistress of the Sea* and lifted its head out of the water. The boat struggled and the people on the deck shouted and stared at the massive tentacle that slithered on board before they ran away in fear, tucking into corners of the deck.

"Turn off your engines and be prepared to be boarded," a man from one of the smaller crafts said through a bullhorn.

The beast looked around and assessed. It wasn't these people it was after.

The mini patrol boats that sped beside the larger boat tried to steer away—that was what the monster was after—but they were too late. The Tupilaq reached its free tentacles out and grabbed the people from the small crafts, held them up, brought them close to its face, roared, tore some in two with its hands, and slammed others on the deck with its tentacles. It tossed them into the ocean, discarding them like trash. Red splatter marks stained the planks, and mangled body parts were scattered about.

The creature roared as *The Mistress of the Sea* killed its engines and began a headlong drift.

The Tupilaq crawled around the boat as if it were looking for something. The massive forty-foot body rocked *The Mistress of the Sea* but showed enough care not to sink it. It looked ahead at the ship's bearing and let go of the boat and slid away gently, leaving the boat.

It remained just below the surface and came upon the Cairn Energy oil rig. The massive steel legs underneath the water were pillars of strength and appeared to be immovable.

The Tupilaq pulled on the legs and lost interest in what was below the surface. Rather, it turned its attention to what was above. It climbed the rusted rig, its body color almost matching the rust. The massive tentacles, hands, and jaws began to dismantle everything on the platform. Communications were torn away; cranes, railings, stairways, and living quarters were crushed. Nothing on the top of the platform was untouched, and all was destroyed by the monster.

When it was done, the creature moved down the destroyed rig and the people on *The Mistress of the Sea* came out of hiding and began to cheer. A crew member took photos with his cell phone, not even thinking to change the phone over to video.

16

A LOOK INSIDE

Illaq waited until Boas and Eko left the room before he took the box out of the duffel bag he brought.

"I don't know what you're up to, and I don't know if I want to know," Illaq said.

Fina took the box. "You don't, and thank you."

"You're welcome." He took his empty duffel bag, folded it, and started to walk out of the room. "I guess."

Fina watched him go and removed the top of the box. Inside were all the necessities: sinew, a square of skin, muskox tusk, hair, and a carving knife that had a little rust on it but was still as sharp as a razor.

Fina covered the box and rested his head. He needed time to think about what he would need to create to try to counter the giant octopus he saw out there. Forty feet, massive tentacles, and incredible speed. That's what he knew about it. The natural enemies of the octopus were sharks, eels, dolphins, and whales.

Fina had to think about what would have the best chance at being able to battle the octopus, overcome its defenses, and kill it. The idea of creating a combination of two species was the best way to go. He would choose the two fiercest adversaries of the octopus he could think of. The killer whale, otherwise known as the orca, had begun to make its way into the waters around Greenland and was a formidable opponent. Orcas had long dorsal fins, which prevented them from coming into the waters because of the ice, but with rising temperatures they were becoming more common.

His second choice was the eqalussuaq, or the gurry shark. Bigger than the great white and a fierce hunter, the combination of the shark and the whale would be perfect. His first step was to create the tupilaq he would call the Killer Gurry Whale Shark. Having been a fisherman most of his life, he knew the anatomy of fish very well. Choosing the best, most durable, and meanest parts was what he needed to do.

He took out his knife and the muskox tusk and began to carve, gently shaving away the dentine and enamel, shaping his creature. The decisions were simple: He would use the body and brain of the orca, highly intellectual animals with complex linguistics enabling them to call upon other orcas. They had pack knowledge, which could be used as an advantage to the massive fish that would top off at around 32 feet long; thick and strong.

He would borrow the fins from the shark to give the orca speed. Pectoral fins, dorsal fins, second dorsal fin, pelvic fin, the caudal keel, and lastly the caudal fin. Orcas move at around four miles per hour, and a shark can move up to 15 mph. But this was no ordinary beast. This was a creation spawned from his imagination and limited only by his vision. It would be fast and mean. The muscle throughout would be thick and strong, making it faster than any shark before. It would have the ability to move so fast it would appear as a blur.

The parts used were just the pieces needed to make this thing right. He would use the rending teeth and sleek face of the shark to help keep it fast and give it an immeasurable biting power.

As Fina carved into the tusk and shaped his design, he started to recite his chant in his head and occasionally deep in his throat so as not to be heard but to give his creation knowledge and power, speed and strength.

He asked his creation to come from the deep and to kill the Tupilaq Octopus. He told it to use its speed and its ferocity to kill and taught it to call out for more orcas to help. The language would be the same between the fish, so they would come, and they would hunt as a pack with the mixed species.

It might take him weeks to perfect his creation. Enough time for him to get out of the hospital and go to the one place where he knew his magic could spread and call forth his creation.

17

FEEDING FRENZY

A 52-foot humpback whale swam at a depth of 500 feet. Its huge, wing-like flippers had knobs on the leading edges. The serrated, 18-foot wide tail waved up and down gracefully.

A quick approach from the Tupilaq Octopus escaped the whale's sense of danger, and it maintained its nine mile per hour heading. The Tupilaq followed the whale, remaining above it, waiting for the right time to act.

The humpback had been under for over twenty minutes and needed to surface for some air. As it began its ascent, it rose right into the waiting arms of the Tupilaq Octopus. The monster sat on the whale's head and covered the two breathing holes near the top of the head.

The octopus then wrapped the massive body of the whale with its thick tentacles. It squeezed the eyes, ears, flippers, throat grooves, and rostrum and dragged the massive creature to the bottom of the ocean floor, held it still, and drowned it.

The Tupilaq Octopus wasted no time getting its fill of meat. It took huge chunks out of the whale's hide with its massive mouth and double rows of teeth, devouring the carcass in less than half an hour. The frenzy clouded the water with blood and attracted nearby gurry sharks. The 18-foot eating machines started to pick on the remains of the body, and the Tupilaq hid in an exposed outcropping of rock, changing its normal color of orange to dark brown so it could rest undetected by all the predators that were near while it digested its food and gathered its strength.

18

TIME PASSES

Fina had been bound to the bed for nearly two and a half weeks before the doctors felt he was ready to go home. They had taught him the importance of how to care for his wound. It was fully closed but still healing, and they warned him of infection. He listened to their every word, remembered every method, and would apply it so he didn't have to worry. He had a job to do and didn't want anything getting in the way of that.

TELE Greenland had finally come forward to the general public with the confirmation that there was indeed the threat of a giant octopus in its waters. They played a grainy fifteen-second clip of a huge orange octopus that dove into the deep and showed a still picture of it climbing an oil rig and dismantling it. The creature was enormous and almost looked fake.

But Fina knew the truth and kept working on his own version of the tupilaq to battle this creature. Meanwhile, the huge octopus continued to attack ships, mostly in Baffin Bay, seemingly in a blind rage to create chaos.

Some ships had been rerouted to go through the future Central Atlantic shipping route. The octopus let nothing through there either, and it seemed from the activity there could have even been more than one of these giant creatures patrolling the seas. The theory arose because the area it covered was huge, and if there was only one, the speed it worked at was incredible. This forced the shipping lanes to strictly use the Northern Sea route.

Undeterred, Fina worked and completed the tupilaq that would destroy the terror of the sea around Greenland. Whether it be one or many, his creation would be stronger, smarter, faster, and an instinctive killer. It wouldn't be focused on anything but hunting the octopus and killing it. The threat would be eliminated and so would the shaman that created it and this chaos.

Boas came into the room. "Are you ready to get home?"

"Like you have no idea. I cannot put it into words," he said. He had his jeans on; the pant leg was pinned up on the leg that was missing. He had on his shirt and needed no help in getting his coat on.

Eko pulled the wheelchair up to the bed and slapped the seat. "Come on, get in. You're out of here."

Fina scooted to the edge of the bed, grabbed the railing of the chair, and sank into the seat.

"Can you grab my bag?" Fina said to Illaq as soon as he entered the room.

Illaq placed the bag in Fina's lap and placed a hand on his friend's shoulder. "Today is the big day."

"It is, guys. I can't wait to get to my place. Nothing like home, you know?" He placed his hands on top of his bag and Eko pushed him out of the room with the escort of a nurse. They got him outside and into the truck, and a pair of crutches went with him.

The guys had hung around for the better part of the day, helping to arrange the house in a way that would help Fina get around easier. They also took things that were up high and lowered them so everything was within reach.

Now that they were gone, Fina went into his yard and walked with the crutches through snow and ice. He reached his shed and removed his sled and reins for the dogs. They all began to bark and show their willingness to pull the sled.

"Not tonight, guys," Fina said. "First light tomorrow we have something very important to do." He fed the eight large Greenlandic huskies. Each had their own fenced-in pen, and as he set the food down, he grabbed each dog and petted its head.

"I've missed you guys," he said and went into the house, made himself something light to eat, and lay down on the couch, the shoebox on the floor right next to him.

"Tomorrow we kill an octopus."

19

FIRST LIGHT

Fina had the dogs all fed, harnessed, and ready to go. Restless to get started and reach their destination, the dogs barked and whined.

He sat in the sled and looked at the tupilaq that was in his right hand, which shook terribly. He had no idea of the power of the shaman who conjured that abomination. But whoever he was and whatever his intention, he was responsible for Fina's missing leg and dead brother. That was enough motivation to take the chance that his creation was better, stronger, and smarter.

He pushed the tupilaq into his pocket, and with confidence he gave the reins a gentle tug and yelled, "Yah!"

The dogs dug their hind legs in deep, pulling the sled, getting up to speed. They barked and snapped at each other but pulled the sled at high speeds. Fina had packed enough supplies to last him and the dogs two full days just in case he ran into any problems.

Fina set a course to the mountainous ice sheet that overlooked the deep ice canyon valley. There was a large rivulet there that carried fast-moving glacial waters. High above that water was where he believed any experienced shaman would go to release his tupilaq—his creation . . . his curse . . . his magic.

The journey would take the better part of half the day. He left early enough that Boas, Eko, and Illaq wouldn't have stopped by yet, so they wouldn't know where he had gone and would be unable to follow. It was of the utmost importance to make sure he kept his friends safe and sheltered from what he was about to do. He didn't want to risk their lives. It was exactly as he had said a few weeks ago in the hospital: This wasn't their fight.

As the large Greenlandic huskies dug deep and ascended the inclines for their master, Fina prayed, repeating it over and over again, forgetting his friends back home, forgetting the consequences of what might happen if this went wrong. He needed to stay focused, to believe in what he created and what he was doing.

Spiritual war was on the horizon, and he needed to put on his armor. He took out the tupilaq and once again made sure its design was perfect. He twirled it in his hand and inspected it close to his eye for the final time. Every detail was as it should be. The dogs almost had him at the top.

His design was genius and his chant, which his creation would abide by, was perfect. He had combined the best parts of the killer whale and the gurry shark to make an efficient killing machine; once done, it would adapt with the orcas and live out its life of about fifty years as one of them.

The dogs stopped and lay down. Fina knew they were close to the edge and it was his turn to act. He climbed out of the sled and held onto the tupilaq he'd named the Killer Gurry Whale Shark. He pulled himself along the snow with his hands, switching the tupilaq from one hand to the other, continuing his chant.

Five minutes and he was looking over the edge, peering down at the fast-moving, crystal clear glacial water. If there was any doubt in this moment, the tupilaq he'd created should be destroyed and he should get back on his sled and head home, leaving the fight to someone else.

But there was no hesitation. He called forth to his creature, asking it to emerge from the deep, to avenge his brother and to kill the giant octopus for the sake of Greenland. He dropped the tupilaq, then watched it hit the water and get pulled along the current.

He'd just waged mystical warfare where not only the life of his creation was on the line, but his was too.

He crawled back to his sled, got the food out of the sack, fed the dogs, and then ate as well. He would head back home this night, hoping he would reach low altitude before sundown.

20

THE KILLER GURRY
WHALE SHARK

Fina's tupilaq rushed through the canyon. Being tossed and twirled by the rushing water, it was pulled under, deep. It reached the Petermann ice shelf, and suddenly the tupilaq came to life and grew right out of the carving. It started out the size of the actual tupilaq that was dropped into the water and went on a feeding frenzy of salmon and halibut, growing at an exceptional rate.

This progression was a show of Fina's shamanistic power. The Tupilaq Killer Gurry Whale Shark turned into a massive, 35-foot killing machine. As it exited the river and made its way into the Arctic Ocean, the Tupilaq began to hunt. It started at the ocean floor and looked for any signs of the octopus.

Hours went by and the Tupilaq Whale Shark finally made its way deep into Baffin Bay, the main body of water the Tupilaq Octopus patrolled.

The Killer Gurry Whale Shark ascended and dove and came upon the carcass of a massive humpback whale. Like a cat seeing a dog, the Tupilaq Octopus rose from its resting spot inside the jagged rocks of the deep, sensing a natural enemy. As it opened itself up, it changed colors: brown, tan, and then orange. The Tupilaq Octopus growled.

Undeterred by the warning growl, the Killer Gurry Whale Shark turned and disappeared into the deep blue, only to turn around and wag its caudal fin, moving water like a giant ship, propelling itself toward the octopus.

The two monsters collided. The octopus grabbed the Killer Gurry Whale Shark and the two wrestled. The Tupilaq Octopus was unable to get a good grasp on the whale shark and found itself at the end of a fierce bite.

The Tupilaq Octopus let go, shot out a large cloud of thick ink, pulled its legs close to its body, and pumped them hard, fleeing into the waters, knowing where it needed to go to beat this thing.

21

MYSTICAL WARFARE

Akutak could feel that his creature was now in combat with another shaman's creation. He was disappointed that his people were unable to put the pieces together that the Tupilaq Octopus was created to protect Greenland, not harm it.

This was it, and Akutak had a bad feeling about what he sensed. He went into his daughter's room, wiped the sweat from his brow, reached into her crib, and took her out. He held her tight, rocked her gently, and looked into eyes that depended on him.

"I love you, Ronja," Akutak said. "If I am never to see you again, I hope your mother never lets you forget who I was and how much you meant to me."

He placed her down, covered her with the animal skin blanket, and exited the room. He entered his bedroom where his precious Sarmok was reading peacefully. It was getting late, and she rested whenever Ronja would let her.

"What is wrong, Akutak?"

He kissed his Sarmok and held his lips to her forehead.

"I must leave at once," he said and sat on the bed next to her.

"Why now, at this time of night? Can't it wait until morning?"

"I'm afraid it can't," he said. "I left something behind during my hunt of the muskox."

"You should wait until daylight comes again. Soon it will be completely dark."

"I know it will, but what I left I must get."

"What is it?"

"Something the ancients gave me," he said. Sarmok knew she couldn't ask what that item might be once he mentioned the ancients. It was secreted in their culture.

She reached out, pulled Akutak close, and held him tightly. "Come back to us," she said and kissed his cheek.

He gave her a smile, got up, and walked out of the room and then out of the house. He walked in the direction of the place where he had taken down the muskox. That would be a good place for him to sit and wait for death to come if his Tupilaq

Octopus were to succumb to whatever creature was placed in the water to dispel his.

A sudden, sharp pain in his side made him fall to his knees. He clamped his eyes shut, leaned forward, and rested his head on the cold ground.

"It is injured," Akutak said. He held his side, found the raised ground where he had hunted, and sat there and looked up at the coming night sky. It was beautiful, and he decided he wouldn't mind seeing his ancestors. He missed his father and his father's father. But he also found himself thinking of Sarmok and Ronja. He didn't want to leave them. He hoped his tupilaq fought with everything it had.

22

BATTLE OF THE DEEP

The octopus pumped its tendrils and the whale shark gained enough on it to take a piece of one of the tentacles. Swimming below the oil rig platform it had destroyed topside, the octopus used its legs to play a game of cat and mouse with the less nimble whale shark.

The shark would spot the octopus and the octopus would hurry away. Momentum carried the large finned predator forward, and the nose of the whale shark slammed into the giant steel legs of the rig. Then the whale shark wiggled its body to correct its course.

Ink filled the water and the whale shark called out to any other orca that might be near. The octopus continued to play its game and tried to figure out a way to mount the large creature that was after it. Mounting it the same way it did the large humpback whale would be the only way to kill it.

The platform beams were like a maze to the two animals. The octopus rested on the ocean floor, flattened itself out, and turned dark brown. The whale shark swam right over top of it.

Three orcas showed up, and the complex communication they used turned the gathering of orcas into a search party. The only way the octopus could now avoid them was to go topside.

It dared to climb the leg of the rig and made it on top of the destroyed platform. It looked down into the crystal clear water and watched the orcas mount their search. They were spreading out, possibly giving it an opportunity to take one out of the game.

When one of the great whales was underneath the octopus, it dropped down on top of it, and with great strength, it squeezed the large mammal. The trapped orca had no air, and from the pressure around its body it couldn't call out. The octopus bit into it over and over again, and blood filled the water. The wounds were enough to kill the whale, but it would take a little time as it nosed down toward the ocean floor.

The octopus went topside again and repeated this hunting technique two more times. All of the called orcas were dead, and the only thing that remained was the Tupilaq Killer Gurry Whale Shark.

The octopus had its own intelligence and waited until the beast of the deep began to look elsewhere for its foe.

That's when the octopus struck. It quietly entered the water and followed the beast from behind, out of the whale's line of sight. With a quick push of its tentacles, it got on top, wrapped its tentacles around the muscular thing, sunk its claws into its flesh, and squeezed and didn't let go.

The octopus hung on as the whale shark tried to shake off the massive creature. But the octopus had him. It slowly climbed the whale shark's head, immobilized the fins, and wrapped its face, clamping its jaw shut, and suffocated its gills.

The powerful whale shark continued to shake and used the exposed rock to try to force the octopus off him. The octopus hit the jagged outcropping and let go, drifting toward the back end of the giant fish. The octopus grabbed its tail with four of its tentacles and dragged the whale shark backward, using its strong remaining four legs to keep a steady pace.

The whale shark tried to get away but was drowning. The fight became less and less until it was dead from taking in too much water through the gills. The giant octopus had drowned its prey and feasted in victory.

23

WHEN ALL IS LOST

Fina arrived home, feeling ill. He hadn't felt well almost half the trip home. Nausea and a feeling of being unsettled tipped him off that his tupilaq was engaged with the octopus and was not doing well.

He had reached the bottom of the mountains by the time he had hoped and led the dogs the rest of the way. Fina penned up the dogs and entered his house, feeling weak. He placed his crutches on the ground and fell onto the couch.

Short of breath, he thought maybe he made the trip too soon after getting out of the hospital. He took off his pants and looked at the stump where his leg had been severed. He went to change the bandages and noticed there was a lot of blood and puss.

Able to reach the phone on the table next to him, he called Illaq in a panic.

"Where have you been?" Illaq said.

"Never mind that for now. I need you to come over. I'm afraid I might be in trouble."

"What sort of trouble?"

"No time, Illaq. Just come."

Fina hung up the phone and saw that his wound, which had been nearly closed, was now fully opened. It bled, and an awful-smelling puss came out of it too. He lay back, biting down hard at the pain. Sweat ran down his face, and he waited for Illaq, hoping he'd get there soon.

Illaq entered Fina's house and saw him on the couch, the blood from his amputated leg easy to see.

"What did you do?"

"I made a tupilaq and sent it into the ocean to kill that octopus."

"You did what?"

"You heard me, Illaq. Don't lecture me, please, I'm in too much pain and I am afraid of what has happened to it."

"The box I brought you . . . what was in it?"

"My tools to make a tupilaq."

"How could you do that to me? If something were to happen to you, I have to live with that."

"That was my choice, not yours. Just love me the way you always have. You are my brother, not related by blood but by friendship. I need your help. I'm scared."

"I've got to get you to the hospital."

Illaq reached down, put an arm behind Fina's back, and the other behind his leg. He picked him up with a great struggle and took him out to the pickup truck. A thick blood trail followed where they went.

Illaq got him into the truck and hurried to the driver's side. He started the car and sped toward the hospital.

"If something is to happen to me, it is your job to find the most powerful shaman in all of Greenland. He will know exactly what to do."

"Nothing is going to happen to you."

"It already has. I'm afraid I did something I shouldn't have done. I hadn't practiced the art in many years, and the man I've gone up against is very powerful."

"Why did you do it?"

"Because the man who made that thing killed my brother . . . turned me into a cripple. If I die, I want you to know the risk was worth it. I have no regrets."

24

BANDING TOGETHER

Boas and Eko came into the hospital room where Fina was half in and out. His leg had been wrapped, and Illaq still wore his friend's blood.

"What happened?" Boas asked.

"How did that turn into an infection?" Eko asked.

Illaq went close to Fina, shook him, and said, "You need to tell them what you did. It is important."

"I made a tupilaq while I laid in this bed. It took me weeks to make and I cast a spell on it. I wanted to create something that would kill the octopus."

"Fina!"

"Don't judge me, Eko. I lost my brother to that thing, and my leg. I have no regrets."

Fina's eyes were heavy and he fell asleep. The three men left his room and went outside the hospital and stood in a tight circle.

"I'm afraid Fina is going to die because of what he's done. If the octopus is to kill his monster, he will surely die."

"No," Boas said. "He will remain alive. Even though he might have gone against a more powerful shaman, he admitted what he has done. That's the only thing that could save him."

"Once this is over, we need to find a shaman. One who can make something to take out that octopus."

Boas remained in silence, contemplating what was going on here. "Let us hope our friend pulls through. One step at a time."

"I don't think we should wait," Illaq said. "We should find this shaman and send something into the water to help whatever Fina created."

"We can't," Boas said. "That's not how it works. It is his creation against the shaman who created the Tupilaq Octopus. Magic against magic."

25

SHAMAN

Akutak remained seated on the mound where he shot the muskox earlier that day. He felt the pain leave his body as the danger his Tupilaq Octopus was in receded. His creation had won, but at the cost of someone else's life. Like him, maybe they had a wife and young child. Maybe they were a good person. Someone he would go fishing or hunting with.

Unsure if the death of the other shaman was instantaneous upon the destruction of their creation, the idea that someone could be suffering because of him—although as well intentioned as his creation was—bothered Akutak.

He only wanted to stop the damaging effects from cargo and container ships that spewed their emissions into the air not too far off the coast of his island . . . his country. He wanted to make sure the oil rig was crippled beyond use.

The ships traveled in the Baffin Bay, poisoning his people and their livestock and eroding the ice off of their shorelines. The drilling that had taken place off the coast could have turned disastrous if the drillers had found oil. What would it do to the ecosystem and fishing industry had it gone wrong and the black goo filled their waters?

From his perspective on this tiny hill, the stars in the sky were bright and the air crystal clear and fresh. Most anyone wouldn't think twice about the night sky because it was just there. But if one were to take a moment and look, they would see brilliant stars, clusters, and some that even winked. For Akutak it was something even more. It wasn't what you could see—it was what you couldn't see. The stars were tangible, bright beams of hope from his ancestors shining down upon him. Yet the emissions were invisible, silent invaders that rained down upon him and his people and poisoned them.

"I'm sorry," he said into the night sky, his heart heavy. As he thought about the man who didn't understand what his tupilaq was up against, he wished there was a way to keep anyone else from making that same mistake. Whether the other shaman was dead or suffering, he didn't deserve it because he was being poisoned by those ships too. So were his friends and family.

Akutak made a wish upon a star, praying to his dead ancestors that the man's life would be spared. Maybe he would even get the chance to explain to him why he did what he did.

There was no mal intent in his magic. Only the idea to protect his country, his family, friends, and people of the beautiful nation of Greenland.

Akutak stood, rubbed his cold hands together, and stuffed them in his muskox coat made by his wife. It was warm. Perfect. Maybe he should have a talk with her, tell her what he had done and seek her counsel.

At one time that thought was unthinkable, but his love was bound by trust and respect. She was a smart woman who dealt with things logically. Unsure if this would ruin his plans or not, he needed to weigh the risk.

Maybe the message had been sent, and the admission, if nothing else, would help alleviate his grieving mind.

He had a ten minute walk home to decide if that was a good idea or not.

26

AWAKENING

Fina's eyes blinked open. They explored the room for a moment to stare, then he moved his eyes elsewhere trying to figure out where he was.

White walls, a window, bright lights above his head, things in his skin and tape holding them in place. He looked at the railing of the bed and struggled to sit up but could only manage to get onto an elbow. He looked at his waist, covered by layers of blanket and the stump where his leg used to be. There was no pain. They must have had him numbed up again.

He moved the blankets aside and saw his stump had been bandaged up and covered so that he couldn't get to it. Thicker, with more tape. There was no blood seeping through the gauze wrapping he knew was underneath.

He put his head back. Whatever was in the drip was powerful. Somehow he was still alive. Weak and a little dizzy, but alive. Had his Tupilaq Killer Gurry Whale Shark killed the giant octopus?

"Welcome back to the world, Fina," a doctor said, entering the room.

Fina watched him. He looked blurry and stretched like he was a human rubber band.

"From what I'm gathering you took your dogs out on a trip. A long trip. The second day after we released you from the hospital."

Fina tried to focus on the man, hear his words, and absorb them.

"You were told to rest. Instead your stunt reopened the grafts and an infection set in." The doctor moved to the door. Fina knew that the infection was as a result of releasing his tupilaq. "What you did was very dangerous, Fina. It almost cost you your life. When you get out of here in a few days, I'd like you to make sure you follow our instructions exactly and rest until you're completely healed."

The stretched man left the room, and Illaq entered right after him. He looked like he was in a fun house mirror, and Fina barely recognized him. Tone of voice helped.

"Boas and Eko are on their way. The doctor was kind enough to call us when you got out of surgery."

Illaq ran his hand on the rail of the bed and he banged on it. "If you ever do something stupid like that again, I'll kill you myself. Do you hear me?"

"Doubt it," Fina managed to say, still in a struggle to focus.

"You shouldn't," Boas said as he came into the room. "Do you even understand why you're still alive?"

"What would possess you to create a tupilaq to try and counter that octopus out there? You were in one of these beds, telling us not to hunt the thing, that it was someone else's fight. What about the equipment we lacked to fight it?"

"It was my fight," Fina said. "That's why. It was my fight, and I think I lost."

"You did lose," Eko said. "Look at you. Is that what a man who wins a fight with a powerful shaman looks like?"

Fina shook his head and the room swayed.

"You told us what you had done, and that's what saved your life. You know that, don't you? If you didn't admit that you would have died."

"Did you seek out another shaman?" Fina said.

"You're not hearing us."

"You just woke up from surgery not too long ago, you look like hell, and all you can think about is whether or not we got a shaman to attack the octopus that nearly killed you twice?"

Eko knocked on his own head. "He's thick. The thickest one of us all."

"I think you were right," Boas said. "This is not our problem. Let someone else figure this out. The thing has been on the news so I'm sure they're sending something out to go after it."

"I'm sure they are," Fina said.

"So let's leave it to them. OK?"

"You need to focus on getting better. No games this time, Fina. Like us, you are out of the fight."

"OK," Fina said.

"That better not just be talk."

"It's not," Fina said. "I could feel the pain of my tupilaq as it was in battle with the octopus. I never want to experience that again. When it died, it was terrible. My skills in magic have faded with time. I should never have thought I could stand up to him."

"We will all agree on that. You should have known that," Illaq said and patted his friend's hand. "We know you were driven by the death of your brother and what happened to you. But this thing is not for people like us to go after."

27

HUNTING THE THREAT

The Danish frigate ship named the *Absalon* had left the dock hours ago and swept the ocean in search of the giant octopus. It dragged dead gurry sharks and bloodied the water.

Loaded with Mark 46 torpedoes that explode before they hit their target, the ship and its captain, named Zoran, and his crew were ready for anything.

Depth charges were also ready in case the octopus came from underneath the mighty ship. Reports stated that was the main approach of the massive octopus that was responsible for shutting down all shipping lanes surrounding Greenland.

The ship trolled at one-fourth throttle and cut through the waters. The crew was serious about the deadly domestic threat in their waters, threatening their land and their way of life. Their captain was a man of few words and little tolerance.

Captain Zoran was growing impatient that no sign of the octopus had appeared. He'd blanketed the waters where the creature had been seen—mainly in the Baffin Bay. He'd even patrolled the waters around the dozens of crippled freight and cargo ships. The eerie view of the ships that were left to drift was like a ship graveyard.

The octopus had attacked anything that tried to assist the vessels in getting to dock.

"Call me in my quarters if we get a hit on anything."

Captain Zoran went into his quarters and looked at a map that hung on a corkboard.

There was superior intelligence to this thing, and he needed to figure out what it was doing. It had attacked an oil rig in Baffin Bay. He placed a pushpin into the map where the attack happened. It had attacked shipping vessels all around the waters surrounding Greenland.

The first reported attack happened here, also in the Baffin Bay. He put a pushpin there too.

Tugs were sent to bring the first crippled ship into dock. The octopus was sending some sort of message that it wasn't going to allow that to happen so it sank the tugs.

Why?

What was this thing up to and where did it come from?

The captain looked for a pattern and didn't see one.

The footage of what had been done to the propellers of the massive boats was shocking and almost unbelievable. At first, he thought it was faked. That metal was hardened, designed to withstand a great amount of pressure. To imagine the strength of a creature that could bend metal like that . . . it was unfathomable. He'd seen the size of the creature, though, as it climbed the oil rig, and it was huge. Forty, fifty feet or maybe even bigger. The thing was fierce.

The attack on the rig was no accident. Clearly the creature was after it. But before it did that, it had climbed a large GreenPeace vessel and left it and its passengers untouched.

The captain also felt that it was no coincidence that the octopus was in hiding from the frigate ship. It probably knew what it was up against and that its presumably soft skin didn't stand a chance against the explosive power of a Mark 46 torpedo or a depth charge.

The captain leaned his hand against the wall, stared at the map some more, and placed a pushpin where all the cargo and container ships had been attacked.

There were dozens, and the map was covered in tacks by the time he was done, with one exception: the top portion of the country was left untouched.

That was curious . . .

This search now as he tried to locate this giant octopus was most certainly a waste of time, the captain surmised. He would radio his commanders and request to call off the hunt and begin using his ship as a means to start towing in the cargo and container ships that were crippled and left afloat to dock in Iceland.

If they called out five frigate ships, they could have the shipping lanes cleared in two or three days.

If they wanted to get this octopus, after the lanes were cleared, they could reopen them and each cargo or container ship would get an escort from a frigate ship that followed a quarter mile back. Once it came out, the Mark 46 would take care of the rest.

Although this monster was intelligent, he doubted it was intelligent enough to figure that out. That tactic, he reassured himself, would certainly draw it out; then they could take their shots and kill it.

28

IN HIDING

The Tupilaq Octopus squeezed its massive body inside the belly of the ship it had made a hole in a few days ago. The massive cargo ship creaked and groaned as it swayed on the harsh surface of the sea. The octopus used its tentacles to stabilize itself and keep completely tucked inside the cavity.

It heard the sounds of the massive ship and its engines patrolling the waters and instinct told it to hide, that it was no match for what had come.

The giant ship hung around for a long while, and the Tupilaq Octopus remained patient—not even hunger would drive it out of its hiding spot. It took the time to rest its wounds from the run-in it had with the Tupilaq Killer Gurry Whale Shark. A formidable foe, but nothing close to the strength, dexterity, and intelligence that its own creator had given. It almost thought like a human.

One of its tentacles was badly injured during the battle it had with the creature. The tentacle was weak, missing the tip, but it was useable. This reprieve and decision to hide close to the surface of the water would give the octopus some much needed time to renew its strength. Rest at this point was important rather than swimming and trying to dodge a hulking killing machine.

The octopus watched sharks, seals, and a large variety of fish swim by. It was tempted to feed, but not enough to move. Safety and survival were its main concerns.

Deep inside the monster, it knew something else would be coming for it. It knew this because that's what its master had taught it. It was expecting something good. It was almost time.

Maybe it was another, similar monster to aid in the master's cause. Its purpose was for the greater good, and the creature knew it was. The threat that was around would go away, and it would resume what it was created to do.

Once it could safely slither out of the ship, it would need to eat. After that, it would be strong enough to seek out its next target.

29

GUILTY CONSCIENCE

Akutak walked in the front door, and his wife, Sarmok, gasped. Relief showed on her face when he opened the door and returned home to her and Ronja, their daughter, and brought her to tears. She thought for sure she would never see him again. She ran to him and hugged him, and he hugged her back.

"How are you?" she asked, pulling back and inspecting his rosy red face.

"I am fine," he said and pulled back his hood and took off his gloves.

"I was so worried about you, Akutak. I thought I lost you."

"I was worried too." Akutak looked toward their daughter's bedroom. "How is she?"

"She's sound asleep."

Akutak smiled. "She's beautiful."

"She looks a lot like your mother."

"I need to talk to you, and I'm afraid this can't wait until morning. Can we sit? Maybe I can have something warm to drink?"

Sarmok took Akutak's hand and led him to the table. She sat him down and went to get him a warm cup of tea.

"I did something that might have hurt someone."

Sarmok stopped but didn't look at him. Whatever it was that he had done, she knew he would never hurt anyone intentionally. She continued to work on getting the tea ready.

"You need to know that I worked on creating a tupilaq in complete privacy for two years. I've put all the magic I know into it, and I released it into the water near the Petermann ice shelf."

Sarmok looked at him. "You've endangered your life by doing that." She placed the cup of tea down in front of him. "That's why you went away, isn't it?"

Akutak didn't need to answer that. Instead, he sipped his tea.

"You went away because there was a possibility you might die because someone sent something after yours? Another shaman had sent a tupilaq, am I right?"

Akutak nodded. "I could feel the pain it was in and understand its fear. It is strong, and we have a bond. It is big . . . I mean very big. But most of all it has intelligence far beyond any creature in the ocean. I've been teaching it for two years everything I know, and it has learned."

"Are you telling me this because you are concerned?"

Akutak drummed his fingers on the mug. His mind raced and he didn't know where to start. The simplest point would be best. "Yes, I'm concerned."

"But you are fine! Your tupilaq defeated the other tupilaq. You are the best shaman in all of Greenland. They can send their tupilaqs and they won't be able to defeat yours."

"Either way, Sarmok, I'm not concerned about that anymore."

Sarmok sat. "What then? Why do you look so concerned?"

"I think I've made it too powerful, taught it too much."

"What do you think it is doing?" Sarmok said.

Akutak shrugged, although he knew the answer. "It's protecting our country. It has been designed to render the shipping lanes useless so they can't spew their poison into our air. It is also supposed to go after the oil rigs and destroy them so they can't dig into our waters and bedrock."

"What type of creature did you create?"

"Something big enough to take down a freighter if it wanted, but it knows not to poison the water with debris."

"What you did," Sarmok said and reached across the table and caressed her husband's hand, "is all for the betterment of the Greenlandic people. Outsiders come by our shores and have made our people sick, deteriorated our ice sheet, put massive metal castles in our waters to drill holes in our ocean floor. I am proud of you and so will the Greenlandic people be if they hear what you've done."

Akutak sat in silence, mulling his wife's words. "Are you suggesting I tell what I've done?"

"Not only tell, but explain why."

Akutak licked his chapped lips. "He may have crippled the fishing industry, too. There may be a lot of people that might not be happy with what I have done."

"Few against many," Sarmok countered. "Casualties of war."

"I suppose . . ."

"Can you call it off? Get rid of the octopus when you want?"

"Of course," Akutak said and reached into the pocket of his coat. He removed another tupilaq made the same way his great ancestors made it: with carved bone, dried and stretched skin, woven hair and sinew. This totem also contained parts from dead children.

"What will you have to do with it?"

"Go past the Petermann ice shelf and place it into the water and conjure my magic with it. The octopus will follow this to where it came from and it will be sealed away forever or until he is needed again."

Sarmok took away the empty teacup and placed it in the wash basin. "I don't think you tell them that part. Make your demands and speak for our people. Save our country from the intruders and hide the fact you have a way to recall it. I think we should make a trip to the mainland in the morning."

Akutak sat in silence again. "No, I will make the trip and send the message. You and the baby are safe here, and that is the way it will be."

"I understand, husband." Sarmok smiled. "Make sure they don't see your face. I wish them to know *of* you, not *who* you are. We shall keep trouble away from our house."

30

CLEARING THE LANES

Captain Zoran of the frigate *Absalon* had called into command to explain that the octopus was nowhere to be found after sweeping the ocean floor. He requested five more frigates to clear the shipping lanes of the dozens of crippled freight and cargo ships and tow them to Iceland. Their heading: the Keflavík naval station where the boats could be repaired.

After the frigate ships were deployed, Iceland agreed to have the ships moved there, so the frigate *Absalon* hooked to the first ship with massive tow chains and pulled it.

The boat followed the *Absalon* with no resistance. The crippled ship with the Tupilaq Octopus hidden inside its belly started the long journey to the Keflavík port.

31

PUBLIC MESSAGE

Akutak met with a man inside the TELE Greenland broadcast building. His face was hidden well as his wife suggested, and he requested a live broadcast to talk to the people of Greenland. He claimed that he was indeed the one who created the massive octopus that had crippled Greenland's shipping lanes, then destroyed the abandoned oil rig, and unfortunately, halted the fishing industry of the local people.

"Why should I believe you?" the skeptical newsman asked. "I've had dozens claiming responsibility for creating that abomination. And why do you hide your face?"

Akutak laughed and pulled out the tupilaq from his pocket. "Because I am a true shaman who practices in the old way. My great ancestors and my magic are strong. Strong enough to kill anyone or anything alive. Land or sea doesn't matter. My magic has no restrictions. If someone knew who I was, they could use what I know, force me to do evil things."

The man's skeptical eye turned into one of curiosity. "What was that?"

"In my pocket?" Akutak said. "Something genuine and powerful. Something I created with my own hands. You should be more worried about what's out in those waters and not what's in my pocket. My magic is a danger to you, too. You and your family."

The man swallowed hard. "I don't mess with magic and want nothing to do with it."

Akutak pulled the hood over his head snugly, his face lost in the darkness. "Then you should do what I'm asking. I'm looking to send a message to the people of Greenland and another message to the world. That is why I created the tupilaq. It is impossible to stop and will continue its rampage until I decide my message has been sent and fully understood. Understood by both the government of Greenland and the people of the world who have no respect for our land and way of life. That's why I'm here. I want to help get that message across a little quicker so we might return to life as normal here.

Wouldn't you like to be the man who helped forge that path?"

The man turned on his heel and ordered the stage to be set for a broadcast on television, radio, and the Internet.

"I ask that this announcement will be live. No interview. Just my words. That's the way it needs to be. The truth, unedited and unscripted. If you agree to this, you will see I am who I claim to be. But I need to get out of here fast to protect my identity and ensure the safety of my family."

The man stared at Akutak. He nodded. "I understand."

After several minutes of chaos, a chair was placed back from the camera, the lights above shined bright, and Akutak was led to the seat. There were no nerves or reservations. His wife had given him sound advice, and she was right; people needed to hear it. He knew how lucky he was to have her and her counsel.

"Are you ready?"

Akutak nodded from deep within his hood. "I am ready."

"In three, two, one." The man pointed at the cameraman.

"I am a native of Greenland and have a bloodline that goes back to the original settlers. I've practiced the old ways of magic as taught by my father and his father and so on."

Akutak shifted in the seat and leaned forward with his elbows rested on his knees, knowing his identity was safe.

"I have worked on creating something to protect our country from the pollution being rained upon us from the shipping lanes. To dismantle the oil rig they are planning on reopening in 2017 or 2019. I forget the date, and right now it is not important. Either way, I say no to drilling in our waters, and I know most of you agree to that too. They've dug six holes in our ocean floor, and I could no longer sit by and watch them desecrate our country for greed. To sit around and watch our people getting sick, dying, our ice eroding, our ground being displaced and desecrated when it should be left alone, is a coward's way out."

He sat back and paused.

"I am the one who created the giant octopus everyone has been talking about. I did it by creating the most intelligent mollusk I could dream up. I set it loose near the Petermann ice shelf and have heard very little of its success as I rarely listen to my radio because of poor reception. But I have other ways of knowing how it is doing. I know it has crippled our fishing industry, and for that I am sorry. Innocent people have died. I never meant for that to happen, and I can only say I'm sorry. It weighs heavily on my heart. But the message needed to be sent. That message is simple and powerful: Leave Greenland alone!

"The beauty that surrounds us is in danger of being destroyed. Maybe not our generation, but the generation after us. It is our duty to make sure that doesn't happen. All Greenlandic people, I challenge you to make a stand. I plead with the leaders of our great nation to do something like I have. I will recall my creation but will not destroy it. I will have it go into hibernation until we need it again. If they do nothing, they will be making the biggest mistake of their lives. That is all I have to say."

Akutak stood and walked away from the bright lights, camera, and microphones, passed the guy he'd spoken to, and strode out the door.

32

PORT

The naval port of Keflavík, Iceland, was packed with crippled ships. Like a graveyard for cars, all the ships needed major repairs before they became mobile again.

The retrieval of the ships took four full days instead of two or three as originally predicted with all of the frigates working around the clock.

The first ship into port hid a secret in its belly, and hunger pulled it out of hiding. It slithered out of the hole, sank to the bottom of the ocean, and looked above. Hulls displaced water so they could stay afloat.

Bearing its two rows of razor-sharp teeth, it found gurry sharks to feed on as well as other fish that swam in groups. With its large mouth opened, it ate schools of fish in one gulp.

After it settled for a little while and digested and felt its strength return, it darted to the hull of a different ship instead of the one it had hidden in before. The octopus banged into it with its mouth open and it clamped down on the hull, ripping a massive hole into the ship's belly. The ship started to take on water, and with no one on board, they couldn't seal and contain the leak. The ship started going under.

In a blind rage, the tupilaq repeated the process over and over again, sinking the ships where they sat crippled. Above the water they shook, sending massive waves onto the dock, sweeping men off their feet, striking fear into their hearts.

Captain Zoran shouted for the frogmen to hurry into suits and take to the waters. He ordered them to hunt the beast with spears that would be shot from spearguns and explode once the target was hit.

Within five minutes, a dozen frogmen were in the water, weapons in hand as the octopus continued its assault on the ships, oblivious to their presence. The men fanned out, keeping a visual on the frenzied octopus that was as large as the ships it attacked and sank.

"I'm not sure these explosives are enough to penetrate the skin of this beast," one of the frogmen said. The men monitoring their progress topside heard him loud and clear.

"If you have a shot, take it. We have to try to at least chase it out of port," Captain Zoran said. "Get it back out into the sea. Maybe it will return to the Baffin Bay. It is destroying the ships, destroying the base."

"You heard the man," the lead frogman said. "Let's move in and get our shots."

33

CALLING IT BACK

Akutak traveled to the same exact spot where he'd released the Tupilaq Octopus into the fast-moving river. It had taken him a few hours to reach his destination after renting a snowmobile instead of his normal route of travel, which was by foot. He couldn't afford dogs, and time was of the essence. He needed to do what he came for and get out as quickly as possible.

He parked the machine, approached the ledge, and chanted his magical prayer over and over again. He released the tupilaq into the water and continued to recite his prayer, repeating it to ensure that what he sent into the waters would come to life and retrieve the Tupilaq Octopus.

Getting back on the machine, he started it up and returned to town so he could return the snowmobile, never stopping his prayer.

The tupilaq Akutak had dropped into the water got pulled beneath the surface and was swished around till it was sucked into the vacant cave the Tupilaq Octopus had emerged from.

Another Tupilaq Octopus emerged from the cave, bright red in color, and it caught the scent of what it was designed to find and retrieve. With eight legs that it pulled close to the body, it pushed them all outward, and the second Tupilaq Octopus hurried along, its movement like a blur, its mission clear, its urgency a priority.

Akutak arrived at the rental facility and returned the snowmobile. He began his journey back home where his wife and child were waiting for him. Getting a ride from strangers all too willing to drive him, the conversation went on about the tupilaq and how excited they were that someone had the nerve to stand up and do something about the current situation.

He was tired and thought of hot tea and couldn't wait to wrap his hands around the warm mug and see the smiles of his wife and daughter once again.

Unbeknownst to Akutak, he was being watched and followed.

34

FROGMEN

The frogmen stayed away from the octopus and kept their depth purposely low. They all had com in their suits, and the lead diver commanded his men.

"Fan out," he said, his voice followed by the hiss of breathing in air. "I want to surround this thing and take some shots upward. Aim for the mouth. That's the softest part and the best bet to get something in there and blow it apart."

All the men responded to their leader's instruction that they understood.

"Move slow. Take your time and don't shoot until you know it's a good one. Your safety is important so be mindful. We may only have one chance at this."

The men encircled the octopus, but the closer they got, the more difficult it became to maintain control of their depth and aim. The eight flailing legs created waves that went far beyond where it was located. It was like a super strong undertow that easily displaced them.

"I'm heading down, lead," a diver said. "I'm beneath it, but I'm getting pushed around by the waves it's making."

"10-4."

The diver dove, the range of his speargun about 13 feet, but he was going to have to chance a long shot and hope the spear had enough drive behind it to carry forward and to its target.

He looked high above and saw the mouth and the massive teeth. The speargun pressed against his shoulder, he took aim. His finger hugged the trigger.

"I'm calling off the shot. I repeat, I'm calling off the shot," lead said. "We can't get close enough, and I don't want an explosive head running rogue on us. There are too many men in the water."

The diver lowered his weapon, disappointed.

"Topside, we can't get close enough to this thing without being slapped with a tentacle or catching its attention or being tossed around by its wake."

"One shot, lead, that's all I want from you," Topside said. "Call your men up."

"Topside, team," lead said.

"Aye," the team responded in unison.

The men went up and the lead stayed down. He kicked his fins as fast as he could, hiding behind a cargo ship that was submerged and slowly sinking. He moved around the massive metal blockade and found where the creature had bitten a hole in the ship. He entered the hole and was about 15 or 20 feet away from the Tupilaq Octopus.

The ship bobbed as it took on more water and started to lose its cargo. It groaned and turned. The lead frogman was out of time. He aimed and shot. The explosive spear glided through the water and headed straight for the target.

In a blur, the spear disappeared, and the wake that was made by the blur turned the ship and trapped the frogman. He didn't see what happened and couldn't report to Topside. His com was damaged and his oxygen tank had a leak in it.

He remained calm and found his way out of the cargo ship. To his surprise, a second Tupilaq Octopus, slightly smaller and red in color, encircled the first octopus and nudged it. The red octopus must have intercepted the spear and snapped it in half or something. It disappeared into the distance and the orange octopus gave quick chase, leaving the Keflavík naval base in shambles.

The four other frogmen found their team leader and brought him topside.

"What did you see?" Captain Zoran asked.

"There's a second octopus down there. It's not as big as the first, but when it came the two left, headed in the direction of Baffin Bay."

"A second octopus?" Captain Zoran said.

"I think the second octopus intercepted the spear I fired. It protected the frenzied octopus. These things have intelligence that far exceeds your ordinary octopus."

"We have news," a naval officer who had joined the conversation said. "The shaman who created the octopus said he was going to recall it. He warned he would not destroy it but put it in a dormant state in case it is needed again."

"Need it for what?"

"To protect Greenland. He doesn't want the shipping lanes to run beside his country. He believes the emissions are making his people sick, melting the ice off the shores."

"So this was about global warming? Pollution?"

"Apparently so."

"Do they know who this man is?"

"No. Only that he's an extremely powerful shaman. They're saying probably *the* most powerful shaman in all of Greenland. He still practices the ancient arts. Although people don't know exactly who they are, it is rumored there are less than a dozen left."

"We will need to get in touch with the Greenlandic government and see what our next moves are going to be."

"Agreed," the naval officer said. "If you'd like to watch his statement, it's being played over and over again on the television and radio. With all due respect, you can't stop him. Your boats are no match for ancient magic."

35

THE CAVE

The bright red Tupilaq Octopus escorted the orange, larger, older Tupilaq Octopus into the cave they had both originally emerged from. The boulder that had shifted when the first octopus was called forth by Akutak was now rolled back into place by a single tentacle.

The red octopus immediately became receptive to the orange octopus. The older octopus extended his modified hectocotylus arm as he approached his younger counterpart. He inserted the arm into her oviduct and released his sperm.

The Tupilaqs were reproducing, expanding their species, something Akutak had taught the female before he conjured her into existence.

36

VISITORS

Akutak was holding his daughter, Ronja, and Sarmok was busy in the kitchen making dinner. It was a long journey home, but he was home, nevertheless. Safe and sound. Tonight they were going to have muskox with a side of potatoes and beets. The house smelt wonderful, and Akutak's stomach growled.

Thump, thump, thump.

"Are you expecting anyone?" Sarmok asked.

"No." Akutak said and went over to his wife. "You need to take her."

"What's going on?"

"I don't know," Akutak said and handed off the baby. He grabbed his hunting rifle, made sure it was loaded, and stood it next to the door where he could reach it quickly. He moved his mouth close to the seam of the door.

"Who is it?" he said but only heard a muffled voice respond. Unsure if that was by design, he decided to ask again. "I said who is it?"

"Someone who would like to have a word with you, Shaman."

The man who spoke had moved his mouth close to the crease of the door where it met the jamb, near where Akutak spoke.

Akutak looked at his wife and ordered her into the hidden shelter beneath the house. He helped her down before he closed the hatch, saying, "Keep her quiet. Even if you have to put your hand firmly over her mouth. You do not come out no matter what you hear."

Sarmok nodded.

Akutak closed the hatch and went to the door. "Why would I allow a stranger in to have a word with me?"

"Because if you don't, we will tell the country of Greenland and all of its people who you are."

Akutak rested his head against the door and gave himself a moment to think. This moment was worse than when his tupilaq was in a fight. He could try to kill the man at the door, but he wasn't alone. Akutak could feel it; he could sense there were at least four. No, there *were* four.

He put on his muskox coat, gloves, and hat and unlocked the door. He swung it open slowly, his left hand reaching out, ready to grab the rifle. He had no doubt he was fast enough to take them all down.

"I don't think you're going to need that," the man said.

It was as Akutak foresaw: there were four of them.

"Need what?"

"That gun you have leaning on the wall just inside that door. You have your hand hovering over it. If we wanted you dead, we would have shot you through your door."

Akutak let his hand fall to his side. "Why are you here?"

"We followed you from the station, watched you drop another tupilaq into the water, and followed you back to where you dropped off the snowmobile. Then we followed you as you hitchhiked your way back home. We watched your home and waited until we were ready to confront you. We wanted to meet you and explain something to you."

Akutak felt clumsy for not making sure no one had followed him from the broadcast station or the mountains around the Petermann ice shelf.

A man looked at him with anger. He was being held up by two of the other men, his one leg missing.

"I'm the first victim of your monster," Fina said.

"I'm sorry," Akutak said.

"Are you sorry that the monster you created killed my brother too?"

Akutak had no words. "That's not what he was created to do."

"So what am I? My brother? Casualties of war?"

Boas stepped forward. "Answer the man."

"Yes, you are. So is your brother, and I'm sorry for it."

"I came here because I wanted you to understand my pain. See it with your own eyes."

"I can never understand your pain," Akutak said. "I can remember sitting on a little hill watching the night sky as our tupilaqs battled. I felt its fear, its pain, and my thoughts shifted to you. I wondered if you had a family like me. I had hoped you admitted it was you who set your creature loose so that you were alive. I wanted to meet you. That is why I admitted what I had done. I suppose it was to draw you out. I suppose I wanted you to find me."

"Well here I am."

Akutak extended a hand. "I'm glad you're alive. I'm sorry things went the way they went. I love my country, and I'm like a soldier who's willing to die for it."

"Me too." Fina said and Eko held onto him. "Are you going to continue to protect Greenland?"

"For as long as I'm alive and as long as she needs protecting. But I suppose that is up to you gentlemen this night, isn't it?"

Fina extended his hand to Akutak's. They shook, and Fina reached forward and hugged the shaman.

"I accept your apology," Fina said. "I understand why you did what you did. "

"Thank you," Akutak said. He reached into his pocket and handed Fina a tupilaq. Fina twirled it in his hand, easily able to see that it had been made the traditional way. "Now that I have met you, the man who was brave enough to take a stand against the Tupilaq Octopus, I can give you what I've worked on for you."

"What is its power?" Fina asked.

"That, what you hold there, is a healing tupilaq. It will help you with your grief, help you accept the loss of your limb, and keep the memories of your brother fond."

Akutak handed him a leather string.

"Wear it around your neck and don't ever take it off."

"I think we misjudged you," Boas said and shook Akutak's hand. So did Eko and Illaq.

"Promise us you will not give up the fight."

"I promise," Akutak said. "It is safe to fish around Greenland now. Please spread the word. I hope life goes back to normal and our government understands what looms deep in the sea if they fail to protect their people and our land."

"Keep us safe. If you ever have to release it again, let us know and we will spread the word."

"How could I find you?"

"We'll be fishing on the boat called *Life's Journey*. We now know what ours is."

The four men turned around and began walking away.

"We are glad to have met you, Akutak. Your secret is and always will be safe with us," one of them called back over his shoulder.

The men walked away and faded into the distance. Akutak went back inside the warmth of the house, locked the door, and opened the trapdoor. He helped his wife and daughter out of the small cellar.

"What was that about?"

"Making amends," Akutak said and paused a long time. "Maybe I'll take another trip to watch the stars tonight and think about what just happened. Pray to the ancestors so I can find some peace."

Sarmok nodded. "That might be good for you to do."

BOOKS BY
KEITH ROMMEL